Collins

Collins

shame about the Boat Race

boat (race) = face

HarperCollins Publishers
Westerhill Road
Bishopbriggs
Glasgow G64 2QT

First Edition 2006
© HarperCollins Publishers 2006
www.collins.co.uk

Illustrations © Salvatore Rubbino

ISBN-13: 978-0-00-724113-2
ISBN-10: 0-00-724113-5

A catalogue record for this book is
available from the British Library.

COMPILED BY: Justin Crozier

Typeset in Martin Majoor's FF Nexus
by Thomas Callan

Printed and bound by Legoprint SPA

ACKNOWLEDGEMENTS
We would like to thank those authors
and publishers who kindly gave
permission for copyright material
to be used in the Collins Word Web.
We would also like to thank Times
Newspapers Ltd for providing valuable
data. All rights reserved.

William Collins' dream of knowledge
for all began with the publication of
his first book in 1819. A self-educated
mill worker, he not only enriched
millions of lives, but also founded a
flourishing publishing house. Today,
staying true to this spirit, Collins
books are packed with inspiration,
innovation, and practical expertise.
They place you at the centre of a
world of possibility and give you
exactly what you need to explore it.

Language is the key to this
exploration, and at the heart of
Collins Dictionaries is language as it
is really used. New words, phrases,
and meanings spring up every day,
and all of them are captured and
analysed by the Collins Word Web.
Constantly updated, and with over
2.5 billion entries, this living language
resource is unique to our dictionaries.

Words are tools for life. And a Collins
Dictionary makes them work for you.

Collins. Do more.

CONTENTS

Introduction

Changing Rhymes for Changing Times

Shame about the Boat Race casts fresh light on an intriguing and underexposed aspect of the English language: rhyming slang. We tend to think of this as a Cockney phenomenon, intrinsically linked to the East End of London, and conjuring images of pearly queens, jellied eels, and chirpy barrow-boys. But while the slang was first recorded in nineteenth-century London, it has always enjoyed a more shadowy existence than that of a simple regional dialect. It has been, at various times, the language of lowlifes, thieves, costermongers, soldiers, sailors, prostitutes, and actors. It crops up in Scotland, Ireland, the US, and – especially – Australia, as well as in its traditional East London manor.

The purpose of rhyming slang is to disguise and obfuscate. It provides a linguistic veil to spare blushes and exclude unwanted listeners in discussions of the dodgy, the dirty, and the downright obscene. It's simple to understand when you're in the know but difficult to penetrate when you're not. For this reason, rhyming slang has thriven in prisons, playgrounds, and in the demimondes of the music hall and theatre. It's alive and well today, not only on the lips of swaggering mockneys and characters in retro-cool gangster films, but as part of our everyday speech.

Rhyming slang allows its speakers to mention the unmentionable in profusion, thus combining earthiness with elegance. By its very nature, it's elaborate and contrived. And part of the joy of using it lies in explaining its mysteries to the uninitiated:

'D'you fancy a coupla britneys?'

'Britneys?'

'You know –britney spears!'

'Britney spears?'

'Beers, you billy!'

'Billy?'

And so on.

Some of the rhyming slang included in Shame about the Boat Race has settled comfortably into the everyday English lexicon: bread, barnet, berk, and Charlie, for example; while other sections of it continue to grow and mutate: britneys, posh'n'becks, and James Blunts. These changing rhymes for changing times highlight the adaptive and slippery nature of rhyming slang. Shame about the Boat Race is the perfect introduction to this lively, bawdy, and humorous part of the linguistic heritage of all English speakers.

HOW TO USE THIS BOOK

Shame about the Boat Race *is designed with easy browsing in mind. Most of it is self-explanatory – you don't have to read the following to enjoy the book but here is some information to help you get the most out of it.*

• *Headwords*

All main entries are printed in red boldface type and are listed in strict alphabetical order:

boracic

• *Full forms*

Many of the headwords are shortened versions of a longer word or phrase. When this is the case, the longer form is shown in brackets directly after the headword:

boracic (boracic lint)

• *Rhymes and definitions*

The headword or its full form often represents a slang or colloquial term, or a word that could be considered offensive. In this case we give the word the rhyme stands for as well as a fuller definition:

boracic (boracic lint) rhymes with *skint*, without money

• *Examples*

An example to illustrate a rhyme's use is given directly after the definition:

boracic (boracic lint) rhymes with *skint,* without money: *I can't go out tonight – I'm totally brassic*

• *Cross references*

Some words have many rhymes, or there may be interesting comparisons to be made with different rhymes. When this is the case, the entry may be cross-referred to another entry. A cross-reference is introduced by a right-pointing chevron and the word 'see':

boracic (boracic lint) rhymes with *skint,* without money: *I can't go out tonight – I'm totally brassic* > *See* **brassic**

• *Etymologies*

An etymology or interesting fact about either the slang or the word it represents is given after most entries:

boracic (boracic lint) rhymes with *skint,* without money: *I can't go out tonight – I'm totally brassic* > *See* **brassic**

> Boracic lint was a surgical dressing made by soaking lint in boracic acid

• A note on labels

As rhyming slang is used to disguise language that can be offensive or derogatory, a guide to rhyming slang must, of course, reflect this. When a term, either the rhyme, the word it represents, or both, could be regarded as particularly offensive – a taboo word, or sexually offensive – it has been labelled as such by a [!]:

barry (barry nash) rhymes with [!] slash, act of urination

There are some terms included that are extremely offensive in terms of race. When this is the case, a note has been included at the entry to warn against its use.

abergavenny penny: *I ain't got an abergavenny*

> Abergavenny is a town in Monmouthshire, Wales.

ace of spades Aids: *'e's been dealt the ace of spades, poor bloke*

acker bilk milk

> Bernard 'Acker' Bilk is a British jazz clarinettist.

adam and eve believe: *Would you adam and eve it?*

adrian quist *Australian* rhymes with [!] *pissed*, drunk: *mate, I was adrian quist last night*

> Adrian Quist (1913–1991) was an Australian tennis champion.

A.I.F. *Australian* deaf

> AIF stands for Australian Imperial Force.

airs and graces horse races

alan whickers knickers

> Alan Whicker is a well-known British broadcaster.

all quiet on the western (*All Quiet on the Western Front*) rhymes with [!] *cunt* **1** female genitals **2** women considered sexually: *'e's out for some all quiet on the western tonight*

> *All Quiet on the Western Front* is the title of a 1929 novel by Erich Maria Remarque (1898–1970).

amster (*Amsterdam*) *Australian* rhymes with *ram*, con-man's assistant: *that fella's the amster for the guy with the patter*

> *Ram*, meaning a swindler's accomplice, is of unknown origin.

andy mcnab taxi cab

> *Andy McNab* is the pseudonym of a former SAS soldier who is now a successful author.

annalise (*Annalise Braakensiek*) *Australian* rhymes with *back, crack, and sack*, cosmetic depilation of the back, scrotum, and the area between the buttocks: *that cloven hoofter's having a bloody annalise tonight*

> Annalise Braakensiek is an Australian model and actress.

apple (*apple fritter*) bitter (beer): *pint of apple, guv*

apples (*apples and pears*) stairs: *I fell down them apples and broke me bleedin' wrist*

april (*April in Paris*) rhymes with *aris*, backside: *nice april* > see aris, bottle

aris (*Aristotle*) rhymes with *bottle*, backside: *plonk your aris down here and we'll chew the fat* > see april, bottle

> *Aris* is short for *Aristotle*, which rhymes with *bottle*, which is short for *bottle and glass*, which rhymes with *arse* – at least in a Cockney accent. This is an ironic instance of the rhyming term sounding very like the original word, which has probably helped its popularity, as a 'mincing', or 'genteelification', of the somewhat offensive *arse*.

artful dodger lodger

> The Artful Dodger is a juvenile pickpocket in Charles Dickens' *Oliver Twist*.

arthur (*J Arthur Rank*) **1** bank: *I'm off down the arthur* **2** rhymes with [!] *wank*, act of masturbation: *'e's in his uncle ted 'aving an arthur*

> J Arthur Rank (1888–1972) was a British film magnate.

attila (*Attila the Hun*) rhymes with 2:1, upper-second honours degree > *see* desmond, douglas, geoff, trevor

> Attila (406–453) was a king of the Huns, known as 'The Scourge of God' for his military exploits.

auntie ella umbrella: *I've gone and come out without me auntie ella*

auntie meg *Australian* keg, especially of beer: *we've got an auntie meg for after the game*

auntie nelly **1** belly: *wouldn't mind a bit of tucker in me auntie nelly* **2** telly: *Anything on the auntie nelly tonight?*

ayrton (*Ayrton Senna*) rhymes with *tenner*, ten

pounds: *Lend us an ayrton, will ya?*

> Ayrton Senna (1960–1994), a Brazilian racing
> driver, was Formula One champion three times
> before his death in an accident that occurred
> during the San Marino Grand Prix.

babble (*babbling brook*) **1** cook: *I couldn't babble a boiled egg* **2** rhymes with *crook*, criminal; crime; to engage in criminal behaviour: *he's been on the babble all his life*

babe (*Babe Ruth*) truth: *that's the pure babe, mate, honest*

> George Herman Ruth (1895–1948), known as
> 'Babe', was a US baseball star.

bacardi (*Bacardi Breezer*) **1** freezer: *stick it in the bacardi* **2** rhymes with *geezer*, man: *How's it going, me old bacardi?*

> *Bacardi Breezer*™ is a brand of alcopop.

backter (*back to front*) rhymes with [!] *cunt* **1** female genitals **2** woman or women considered sexually

New and old

In general, it's possible to distinguish between two sorts of rhyming slang: we could call these categories 'live' and 'decayed'. 'Live' slang means what it says; it can be used in exactly the same way as the word or words with which it rhymes. 'Decayed' slang, on the other hand, has settled into the sediment of the language and taken on a different character, leaving only an outline of its former meaning, and with the rhyme often largely forgotten.

Sometimes this shift in meaning has been quite subtle. **Barnet,** for instance, seems a simple enough example of 'live' rhyming slang: *Barnet Fair = hair*. But on closer examination, *barnet* isn't used in the same way as 'hair'. For a start, *barnet* is often used in the plural form: *they've got the worst barnets I've ever seen*, for example. Additionally, the singular form usually takes an article: *she's got a nice new barnet*. So *barnet* has really come to mean 'haircut', 'hairstyle', or 'hairdo', rather than simply 'hair'.

In the same way, **berk** has come a long way from its original meaning. Not only has it lost the sting of its original rhyme, but it's also changed in pronunciation, from *bark*, as in *Berkeley*. Today it's a commonplace word, and one that is unlikely to cause a great deal of offence.

Berk is now part of the English language in its own right, whereas its partner in rhyme, **all quiet on the Western,** remains 'live', with its power to shock fully intact – despite the fact that it's used far less often than *berk*.

bacon (*bacon rind*) blind

bacons (*bacon and eggs*) legs: *nice pair of bacons over there*

bag (*bag of sand*) rhymes with *grand*, a thousand pounds: *that geezer owes me a bag*

bag of yeast priest

baked bean rhymes with [!] *queen*, gay man: *'Im? 'E's a flamin' baked bean*

baked beans jeans

baked potato see you later: *baked potato, alligator*

> In a Cockney accent, 'potato' is pronounced *patʌyta*.

bale (*bale of hay*) rhymes with *gay*, homosexual: *Didn't you know 'e's bale?*

ball and bat rhymes with [!] *twat* **1** female genitals **2** girl or woman considered sexually

3 foolish or despicable person

ball of chalk walk: *Why don't you take a ball of chalk, sunshine?*

bangers (*bangers and mash*) cash > *see* sausage

barclays (*Barclays Bank*) rhymes with [!] *wank*, act of masturbation: *you're talking total barclays there mate*

bargain (*Bargain Hunt*) rhymes with [!] *cunt*, mean or obnoxious person: *he's a right bargain, that bloke*

> *Bargain Hunt* is a BBC daytime TV programme, originally hosted by David Dickinson.

barnaby (*Barnaby Rudge*) judge: *this barnaby's a total berk*

> *Barnaby Rudge* is the title of an 1841 novel by Charles Dickens.

barnet (*Barnet Fair*) rhymes with *hair*, haircut, hairstyle, or hairdo: *bit of a dodgy*

barnet there, mate

Barnet Fair was held twice-yearly from 1588 until 1881, and continues to be held once a year at Barnet (formerly in Hertfordshire, now North London). In the Victorian era, it was the largest cattle market in England, and also offered three days of horse-racing. It was thus a major event for the townspeople of London, and was immortalized in rhyming slang while the fair was still at its height in the nineteenth century.

barn owl row: *'ad a right barn owl with the missus last night*

The rhyme of *barn owl* with *row* depends on the Cockney accent, in which the final *l* isn't pronounced.

barry (*Barry Crocker*) *Australian* rhymes with shocker, shockingly bad thing or performance: *he had an absolute barry, mate*

Barry Crocker is an Australian singer (born 1935), who is best known for singing the *Neighbours* theme tune and for songs such as *My One-Eyed Trouser Snake.*

barn owl = row

barry (*Barry Nash*) rhymes with [!] *slash*, act of urination: *I'm bursting for a barry*

> There is a distinct possibility, however, that the term refers to the architects of Trafalgar Square, Charles Barry and John Nash.

barry white rhymes with [!] *shite*, rubbish; nonsense: *turn that off – it's barry white*

> Barry White (1944–2003), the 'Walrus of Love', was a soul singer renowned for his deep voice and prodigious girth.

basil (*Basil Fawlty*) balti: *Let's go for a ruby – how about that basil place near you?*

> Basil Fawlty is the irate hotelier played by John Cleese in *Fawlty Towers*.

bath bun son

battle (*battle cruiser*) rhymes with *boozer*, pub: *Going down the battle tonight?*

beechams (*Beecham's Pill*) **1** bill **2** still (photograph)

Beecham's Pills were a brand of nineteenth-century laxative.

bees (*bees and honey*) money: *'Ow much bees 'ave you got on you?*

belindas (*Belinda Carlisles*) piles (haemorrhoids): *me belindas are really playing up today*

Belinda Carlisle is a singer and member of US rock group The Go-Go's, and had a number of solo hit records in the late 80s and the 90s.

bengal lancer chancer

berk (*Berkeley Hunt*) rhymes with [!] *cunt*, foolish person: *my brief said: 'Sit down, you berk, he's only going to fine you'* > *see* charlie

The Berkeley Hunt, held in Gloucestershire, dates from the eighteenth century. *Berk* is sometimes said to be a contraction of Berkshire Hunt, the 'Old Berks', which has been held since 1830, but the existence of variations such as 'Sir Berkeley' and 'Lady Berkeley Hunt' indicate that the Berkeley Hunt was the original choice of rhyme. Interestingly, *berk* is used as a mild insult in contemporary English, with most users unaware of its origins. In general usage it's no stronger than 'fool'.

berlins (*Berlin Walls*) rhymes with [!] *balls, testicles: he got hit right in the berlins*

billie (*Billie Piper*) windscreen wiper: *my billies ain't working*

Billie Piper is a British actress and pop singer.

bill wyman hymen: *Virgin? Don't think so, mate. Not a bill on 'er.*

Bill Wyman was the bass player in the Rolling Stones between 1962 and 1991.

billy (*Billy Hunt*) rhymes with [!] *cunt,* foolish or despicable person: *don't be such a billy* > see charlie

Like Charlie Hunt, Billy doesn't appear to have been a real person. It's possible, however, that this rhyme arises from the term *billy-hunting*, which referred to both trading in used or stolen metal, and stealing handkerchiefs.

billy wright rhymes with [!] *shite*, rubbish; nonsense: *enough of your billy wright*

> Billy Wright CBE (1924–1994) was captain of the England football team, and was the first player to earn 100 caps for England.

bird (*birdlime*) rhymes with *time*, prison sentence: *I did me bird – I'm straight now*

blind (*blind mice*) ice: *I'll have a winona with blind, thanks*

blood (*blood red*) rhymes with *head*, fellatio: *she gives blood an' all*

blunnie (*Blundstone boot*) *Australian* rhymes with *ute*, utility vehicle: *throw your bag in the blunnie and I'll give you a lift*

> Blundstone Footwear is a Tasmanian company famous for its elastic-sided boots.

boat (*boat race*) face: *nice april, shame about the boat*

boat (race) = face

bolt (*bolt the door*) rhymes with *whore*, prostitute or promiscuous woman: *it was full of scraggy old bolts*

boom (*boom and mizzen, boom and sail*) prison, jail: *'e's back in the boom*

> *Boom and mizzen* and *boom and sail* are nautical terms referring to parts of a ship. Felicitously, these synonymous phrases rhyme with the synonyms *prison* and *jail*.

boracic (*boracic lint*) rhymes with *skint*, without money > *see* brassic

> Boracic lint was a surgical dressing made by soaking lint in boracic acid.

boris (*Boris Karloff*) cough: *nasty boris you've got there, mate* > *see* darren gough

> Boris Karloff (real name William Henry Pratt, 1887–1969) was a British actor best known for his horror-film roles, such as Frankenstein's monster.

bottle (*bottle and glass*) rhymes with [!] *arse*,

backside

bowler (*bowler hat*) cat

brace (*brace and bits*) rhymes with [!] *tits,* breasts: *nice brace*

> As well as rhyming, this is also a play on *brace* meaning 'pair'.

brad (*Brad Pitt*) **1** rhymes with [!] *shit,* act of defecation: *I've got to take a brad* **2** rhymes with [!] *tit,* breast: *look at the brads on that* **3** rhymes with *fit,* physically attractive: *he's well brad*

> Brad Pitt is a US actor renowned as a heart-throb.

bradford (*Bradford City*) rhymes with [!] *titty,* breast > *see* bristol

brahms (*Brahms and Liszt*) rhymes with [!] *pissed,* drunk: *I was a bit brahms last night*

brass (*brass nail*) rhymes with *tail,* prostitute: '*Is that 'is wife?' 'Nah, she's a brass*'

bolt
brass

Tail was common slang for a prostitute in the eighteenth and nineteenth centuries, though it was later used more generally for a woman or women considered sexually. In its earlier sense, *tail* is probably a shortening of *flashtail*, an eighteenth-century term for prostitute, alluding to the display of wares associated with the profession.

brassic (*boracic lint*) rhymes with *skint,* without money: *I'm totally brassic* > *see* boracic

Boracic lint was a surgical dressing made by soaking lint in boracic acid.

brass tacks facts: *the defence lawyer got down to brass tacks*

bread (*bread and honey*) money

bread and butter gutter

bricks and mortar daughter

bristol (*Bristol City*) rhymes with [!] *titty,* breast: *nice pair of bristols* > *see* bradford

britneys (*Britney Spears*) **1** beers: *Fancy a couple of britneys after work, then?* **2** ears: *seen the way his britneys stick out?* **3** rhymes with [!] *queers*, homosexual men: *they're all britneys in there*

> Britney Spears is a US pop singer.

brixton (*Brixton Riot*) diet: *better not – I'm on a brixton*

> The Brixton Riots were large-scale disturbances that took place in South London in 1981, 1985, and 1995.

brown bread dead

bubble (*bubble and squeak*) Greek: *you know, the bubble – Prince Philip*

> Bubble and squeak is a dish of leftover boiled cabbage, potatoes, and sometimes cooked meat fried together.

bull (*bull and cow*) row: *I 'ad a massive bull with me pitch on Monday*

bunsen (*bunsen burner*) earner: *that club's been a*

nice little bunsen for him

burnt (*burnt cinder*) window

> *Burnt cinder* rhymes with the Cockney
> pronunciation of 'window', *winder*.

burton (*Burton-on-Trent*) rent: *I don't know how
I'm gonna pay me burton, I'm that brassic*

> Burton-on-Trent, or more properly, Burton-
> upon-Trent, is a town in Staffordshire.

butcher's (*butcher's hook*) **1** look: *take a butcher's at
that* **2** *Australian* rhymes with *crook*, ill or
injured: *nah, he's not playing – he's butcher's*

calvin (*Calvin Klein*) wine: *I fancy a night in wiv me
plates up and an aris of calvin*

> Calvin Klein is a US fashion designer.

captain cook *Australian* **1** look: *let's have a
captain cook* **2** rhymes with *crook*, ill or injured: *I
was captain cook all last week* **3** book: *always got
his nose stuck in a captain cook*

Captain James Cook (1728–1779) was an English explorer who discovered and claimed the east coast of Australia for Great Britain.

carpet (*carpet bag*) rhymes with *drag*, imprisonment: specifically a three-month prison sentence: *I only got a carpet off that barnaby*

Drag appears originally to have referred to the crime of stealing a vehicle, or 'drag', (either horse-drawn or motorized), for which three months was apparently the expected sentence.

cash (*cash and carry*) marry: *she got cashed again last year*

chalfonts (*Chalfont St Giles*) piles (haemorrhoids): *I'm a slave to me chalfonts – terrible trouble they gives me*

Chalfont St Giles is a village in Buckinghamshire.

chalk (*Chalk Farm*) arm: *'e's gone and broken his chalk*

Chalk Farm is an area in the London borough of Camden.

charley (*Charley Chase*) *Australian* race: *You going down the charleys tomorrow?*

> Charley Chase (1893–1940) was a US comedian and film director.

charlie (*Charlie Hunt*) rhymes with [!] *cunt*, foolish or contemptible person: *'e's a right charlie* > *see* billy

> If any specific Charlie Hunt was the source of this term, his details are now unknown. Interestingly, *charlie*, like *berk* is used as a mild insult in contemporary English, with most users unaware of its origins. In general usage it's no stronger than 'fool'.

charlie (*Charlie Wheeler*) *Australian* rhymes with *sheila*, woman: *come on, mate – there'll be loads of charlies there*

> Charles Wheeler (1881–1977) was an Australian painter who was famous for his female nudes.

chevy (*Chevy Chase*) face: *Of course 'e's lying! Look at 'is bleedin' chevy!*

The Ballad of Chevy Chase is a famous poem about a hunting party ('chase') that results in a skirmish in the Cheviot ('Chevy') hills on the Scottish–English border. The events described are possibly based on the Battle of Otterburn (1388).

chew the fat rhymes with *have a chat,* talk idly or gossip: *we were in the battle chewing the fat*

china (*china plate*) rhymes with *mate,* friend: *listen, me old china, you've got nothing to worry about*

chunder (*Chunder Foo*) originally Australian rhymes with *spew,* vomit: *I was chundering my guts up all night*

Chunder appears originally to have been short for *Chunder Foo of Akim Loo,* a cartoon character created by the Australian artist Norman Lindsay to advertise Cobra boot polish, and then ran in the Sydney *Bulletin* from 1909 to 1920. Chunder Loo was an Indian gentleman who was accompanied by an identically dressed koala.

Who are the Cockneys?

The Cockneys are the group most closely associated with rhyming slang. The traditional definition of a Cockney is someone born within the sound of Bow bells; that is, within hearing distance of the bells of the church of St Mary-le-Bow in Cheapside, in the City of London. More generally, the term is used to describe working-class Londoners, and especially those from the East End.

While we might nowadays associate Cockney modes of speech with gangsters and hardmen, the term has its origins in a view of townspeople as soft and effeminate. The term was originally *cokene ey*, or 'cock's egg', a word that was applied to small or malformed eggs on the mistaken assumption that these had been laid by cocks rather than hens. From there the sense was extended to overindulged or coddled children, the inference being that small or weak children would be indulged by their parents. So a 'Cockney' was originally a spoilt weakling; it was then used as a derisive insult to townspeople in general, contrasting their supposed effeminacy with the strength and virility of country folk.

As so often happens, what was once an insult was reclaimed as a badge of pride. Gradually *Cockney* came to mean a

Londoner rather than an inhabitant of any large town, and later Londoners began to assert their Cockney identity through the music hall and phenomena such as the pearly kings and queens.

claire rayners trainers: *those claire rayners cost 'im a ton*

> Claire Rayner OBE is a British journalist and agony aunt.

clickety-click sixty-six

> This is a term used in bingo.

cloven hoofter *Australian* rhymes with [!] *poofter,* gay man

cobblers (*cobblers' awls*) rhymes with [!] *balls,* nonsense: *that's a load of cobblers*

> An awl is a pointed tool used for piercing leather.

cocoa say so: *I should cocoa!*

> *Cocoa* is used almost exclusively in the exclamatory phrase 'I should cocoa!'.

corned beef *Scottish* rhymes with *deif,* deaf: *he'll no hear you – he's corned beef* > *see* side of beef

> This rhyme depends on the pronunciation of 'deaf' as *deif* in some Scottish dialects.

cream-crackered rhymes with *knackered*, exhausted: *not tonight, Josephine – I'm cream-crackered*

currant bun The Sun (a British newspaper)

custard (*custard and jelly*) telly

daft (*daft and barmy*) army: *'E's that bleedin' stupid e's gone and joined the daft!*

daisy (*daisy root*) boot: *get yer daisies on, then*

dame edna (*Dame Edna Everage*) Australian beverage, drink, often an alcoholic one: *Fancy a few dame ednas tonight?*

> Dame Edna Everage is a character created by the Australian comedian Barry Humphries.

darby or **derby** (*Darby Kelly, Derby Kelly*) belly: *we'd better get something in our darbies before we go down the rubbity*

> Darby Kelly is a character who appears in several traditional ballads and music-hall songs.

dark and dim swim

darren gough cough > *see* boris

> Darren Gough is a former England test cricketer.

desmond (*Desmond Tutu*) 2:2, lower-second honours degree > *see* attila, douglas, geoff, trevor

> A pun rather than a conventional piece of rhyming slang, this term namechecks the South African archbishop and veteran anti-apartheid campaigner.

diana dors rhymes with *all the fours*, forty-four

> Diana Dors (1931–1984) was a British film actress. This term is used in bingo.

dickory (*dickory dock*) rhymes with *clock*, meter in a taxi-cab: *Hickory dickory dock.* > *see* hickory

> Hickory dickory dock is a nursery rhyme that describes a mouse's ascent and descent of a clock.

dicky (*dicky bird*) word: *she didn't say a dicky about it*

cream-crackered
dicky

dog & bone = phone

dicky (*Dicky Dirt*) shirt: *stick on a whistle and a smart dicky for the big day tomorrow*

> Dicky Dirt appears to be a name invented for the rhyme, playing on an earlier term, *dicky*, for a shirt or shirt front.

didn't oughter daughter: *Have you seen his didn't oughter?*

ding-dong sing-song: *we had a bit of a ding-dong round the joanna*

dog and bone phone: *I was on the dog and bone to me mother the other night*

doris (*Doris Day*) rhymes with *gay*, gay man: *'e's a doris*

> Doris Day is a US singer and actress, best known for her film roles of the 1950s and 60s.

douglas (*Douglas Hurd*) **1** rhymes with *third*, third-class honours degree > *see* attila, desmond, geoff, trevor **2** rhymes with [!] *turd*, piece of

excrement

> Douglas Hurd was British Foreign Secretary from 1990 to 1995.

d'oyly carte rhymes with [!] *fart*, emission of intestinal gas from the anus, esp an audible one: *that was some d'oyly carte he let rip in there*

> Sir Richard D'Oyly Carte (1844–1901) was a British theatre producer who founded the D'Oyly Carte Opera Company to produce the operettas of Gilbert and Sullivan.

duchess (*Duchess of Fife*) wife: *And 'ow's the duchess?*

> *Duchess* appears to have been simply a mock-flattering or ironic term for a woman or wife before acquiring its rhyme.

dukes (*Duke of Yorks*) rhymes with *forks*, fists: *Put yer dukes up!*

> *Forks* is slang for fingers.

dutch (*Dutch plate*) rhymes with *mate*, friend; wife: *there's no-one like me old dutch*

Dukes (Duke of York) = fists

eartha kitts rhymes with [!] *tits*, breasts: *you can see her eartha kitts*

> Eartha Kitt is a US singer and actress, known for playing Catwoman in the *Batman* TV series.

eau de cologne *Australian* telephone

edgar britt *Australian* rhymes with [!] *shit*, act of defecation: *gotta take an edgar britt*

> Edgar Britt was an Australian jockey.

edinburgh fringe rhymes with [!] *minge* **1** female genitals **2** women collectively considered as sexual objects: *there'll be plenty of edinburgh fringe about, I can tell you*

> The Edinburgh Festival Fringe is the world's largest arts festival.

elephants (*elephant's trunk*) drunk: *I was elephants last night*

emma freuds haemorrhoids: *I've 'ad terrible trouble with me emma freuds*

elephants (elephant's trunk) = drunk

Emma Freud is a British broadcaster.

enoch (*Enoch Powell*) towel: *remember your enoch for the fatboy slim*

> Enoch Powell (1912–1998) was a British politician.

ethan (*ethan hunt*) rhymes with [!] *cunt*, mean or obnoxious person: *what an ethan he is*

> Ethan Hunt is the hero of the *Mission: Impossible* films, and is played by Tom Cruise.

everton (*Everton toffee*) coffee: *pop round for an everton some time*

> Everton is a area in Liverpool, from where the lemony toffee hails.

eyes front rhymes with [!] *cunt* **1** female genitals **2** women considered sexually: *plenty of eyes front about tonight*

farmers (*Farmer Giles*) piles (haemorrhoids): *'e can't sit down on account of 'is farmers*

> Giles is an archetypal name for a farmer.

fatboy slim gym: *I'm staying in – I'm cream-crackered after the fatboy slim*

> Fatboy Slim, aka Norman Cook, is a British dance musician and DJ.

fiddley-did quid (£1): *Lend us a fiddley-did, will ya?*

field of wheat street: *'e lives on the same field of wheat as me didn't oughter*

fisherman (*fisherman's daughter*) water: *I'll take a spot of fisherman in the whisky, thanks*

flingel (*Flingel Blunt*) rhymes with [!] *cunt*, contemptible person: *I can't stand that flingel*

> 'The Rise and Fall of Flingel Blunt' is an instrumental record by The Shadows.

flowery (*flowery dell*) prison cell: *'e won't be bothering anyone while 'e's banged up in 'is flowery dell*

four by two rhymes with *Jew*, Jewish person: *her*

boyfriend's a four by two from Golders Green (This is highly offensive.)

four-wheel skid rhymes with *Yid*, Jewish person (Both *four-wheel skid* and *Yid* are highly offensive terms.)

frank hyde *Australian* wide (in cricket, a bowled ball that is outside the batsman's reach and scores a run for the batting side)

> Frank Hyde is an Australian former rugby league player and commentator.

friar (*Friar Tuck*) rhymes with [!] *fuck* **1** tire or exhaust: *I'm totally friared* **2** copulate with

> Friar Tuck was one of Robin Hood's Merry Men.

frog (*frog and toad*) road: *time to hit the frog*

gary (*Gary Glitter*) rhymes with [!] *shitter*, anus: *he takes it up the gary*

> Gary Glitter is the stage name of Paul Gadd, a 1970s glam-rock star.

frog (& toad) = road

gary player rhymes with *all-dayer*, all-day drinking session: *we was on a gary player yesterday*

> Gary Player is a South African golfer who was widely regarded as one of the best players in the world.

geoff (*Geoff Hurst*) **1** rhymes with *first*, first-class honours degree > *see* attila, desmond, douglas, trevor **2** thirst: *let's go down the battle – got a bit of a geoff on me*

> Sir Geoffrey Hurst MBE is an English footballer who scored a hat-trick in England's 1966 World Cup Final victory over Germany.

george bush rhymes with *mush*, face: *I couldn't believe the look on his george bush*

> *Mush* is a slang word for face.

george moore *Australian* four (in cricket, four runs scored off a shot that hits the ground once before crossing the boundary): *we need a george moore off the next ball*

George Moore was an Australian champion
jockey.

georgie bests breasts: *quite a set of georgie bests on*
her

> George Best (1946–2005) was a celebrated
> footballer for Manchester United and Northern
> Ireland.

germaine (*Germaine Greer*) beer: *'e's been on the*
germaines all night

> Germaine Greer is an Australian feminist writer
> and broadcaster, author of the *The Female*
> *Eunuch.*

germans (*German bands*) hands: *Keep your*
germans to yourself!

gianluca (*Gianluca Vialli*) rhymes with *charlie,*
cocaine: *there was bleedin' gianluca all over the table*

> Gianluca Vialli is an Italian footballer and
> manager.

ginger (*ginger beer*) rhymes with [!] *queer,* gay
man: *that bar's full of gingers*

Down under

While rhyming slang is often thought of as a London, and specifically Cockney, phenomenon, it has long been a thriving part of Australian English, where it has become a recognizable part of everyday speech.

A great deal of Australian rhyming slang is identical to its British counterpart, no doubt because much of it arrived with nineteenth-century migrants and deportees. But the slang has put down roots in Australia, not least because of the informality of Australian English and its consequent wealth of slang of all kinds. There are interesting equivalents to

Cockney terms, as with **goanna** and **joanna,** both of which rely on idiosyncrasies of the two accents to rhyme with 'piano'.

Naturally, Australian rhyming slang reflects the country's culture. The central position of sport in Australian life is reflected in terms such as **dropkick** and **high diddle diddle,** while other rhymes incorporate the names of well-known sportsmen such as **Mal Meninga** and **Ron Coote.** Other rhymes reflect Australia's history, flora and fauna, and placenames: **Ned Kelly, Captain Cook, mallee root, goanna, Kirribilli,** and **Werris Creek.**

Some might also say that there's a

typical Australian bloody-mindedness in terms like **cloven hoofter,** which was invented purely to achieve a rhyme!

ginger meggs *Australian* legs: *nice ginger meggs over there*

> *Ginger Meggs*™ is a long-running Australian cartoon strip, which first appeared in 1921.

goanna *Australian* piano: *Give us a tune on the old goanna* > *see* joanna

> A goanna is an Australian lizard; the word itself is a corruption of *iguana*, and rhymes with *pianna*, an Australian pronunciation of 'piano'.

god forbid 1 rhymes with *kid*, child: *I've got to look after me skin and blister's god forbids tonight* **2** rhymes with *Yid*, Jewish person (Both *Yid* and this sense of *god forbid* are highly offensive.)

god love 'er mother: *got to visit the god love 'er*

> This rhyme depends on the Cockney pronunciation of 'mother' as *muvva*.

goose and duck rhymes with [!] *fuck*, act of sexual intercourse: *got a goose and duck last night*

grass (*grasshopper*) rhymes with *shopper*, person

who informs the police about a criminal activity

green (*greengage*) stage: *Darling, I bestride the green like a colossus!*

greengages wages: *I get me greengages Friday so I'm up for a gary player Saturday.*

gregory (*Gregory Peck*) neck: *look at the size of that geezer's gregory*

> Gregory Peck (1916–2003) was a US actor; his films include *The Big Country* and *To Kill a Mockingbird*.

grumble (*grumble and grunt*) rhymes with [!] *cunt* **1** female genitals **2** women considered sexually: *'e got a bit of grumble last night*

gypsy (*gypsy's kiss*) rhymes with [!] *piss*, act of urinating: *hang on a mo – I need a gypsy*

haddock (*haddock and bloater*) rhymes with motor, car: *that's a flash haddock*

> 'Haddock and bloater' is one of many rhyming

phrases that use two related words or two words from the same semantic field - in this case, the names of two fish.

half-inch rhymes with *pinch*, steal

ham (*ham and beef*) rhymes with *chief*, chief prison warder: *the ham's a right sherman – best keep your nose clean*

hampsteads (*Hampstead Heath*) teeth: *'e got 'is hampsteads knocked out in a scrap*

> Hampstead Heath is a large area of parkland and woods in North London.

hampton (*Hampton Wick*) rhymes with [!] *prick*, penis: *'e does 'is thinking with 'is 'ampton*

> *Wick*, meaning penis, forms the basis of the phrase 'dip one's wick', which means 'to have sexual intercourse'.

hank marvin starving: *I'm bloody hank marvin* > *see* lee marvin

> Hank Marvin is the lead guitarist of The Shadows.

harry (*Harry Randall*) candle: *she can't 'old an 'arry to 'er old mum*

> Harry Randall (1860–1932) was a music-hall comedian and pantomime dame.

harry tate state (of untidiness or anxiety): *I was in a right 'arry tate before we got started*

> Harry Tate was the stage-name of the music-hall comedian RM Hutchison (1872–1940).

hearts (*hearts of oak*) rhymes with *broke*, without money: *no can do – I'm hearts at the minute*

hey diddle diddle 1 middle **2** rhymes with *piddle*, urinate

hickory (*hickory dickory dock*) rhymes with *clock*, meter in a taxi-cab: *forget the hickory – let's call it twenty squid all in* > *see* dickory

> *Hickory dickory dock* is a nursery rhyme that describes a mouse's ascent and descent of a clock.

high diddle diddle *Australian* middle (of

52

Australian Rules or rugby goalposts): *he kicks it right through the high diddle diddle*

hit or miss rhymes with [!] *piss*, urinate act of urinating > *see* miss or hit

hot beef stop thief!: *Hot beef! Hot beef! That geezer's half-inched me wallet!*

inky smudge *Australian* judge

irish (*Irish jig*) wig: *this geezer's wearing an irish*

iron (*iron hoof*) rhymes with [!] *poof*, gay man

jack (*Jack Jones*) own: *I'm on me jack down here*
> Jack Jones is an American jazz singer.

jack in the box rhymes with *pox*, sexually transmitted disease: *'e got the jack in the box off a brass*

jack scratches *Australian* matches: *Got any jack scratches?*

jack sprat fat: *'Ow jack sprat is the lemon with the fancy barnet?*

> Jack Sprat is the nursery-rhyme character who 'could eat no fat', making this a somewhat ironic rhyme.

jack the ripper 1 kipper: *a nice jack the ripper for breakfast* **2** stripper: *she works as a jack the ripper at his club*

> The first rhyme features a rather macabre joke: to make kippers, herrings are cut open and eviscerated, in a similar manner to the victims of Jack the Ripper, the notorious perpetrator of several unsolved murders in London in 1888.

james blunt rhymes with [!] *cunt*, mean or obnoxious person: *you're a james blunt, sunshine, and that's all there is to it*

> James Blunt is a British singer-songwriter.

jam jar car: *not a bad-looking jam jar, that*

jam tart heart: *'e's got a dodgy jam tart*

54

Ghosts of the past

An intriguing aspect of rhyming slang is the way in which it preserves the names of people and practices that are otherwise forgotten. There's a whole host of faded stars of stage, screen, and sports who are still remembered in rhyming slang – Oscar Ashe, ZaSu Pitts, Kate Carney, and Tod Sloane, for example.

Rhyming slang also preserves elements of other kinds of slang: *forks* for fingers, as in **dukes** (Duke of York = fork), or *gamahuche* in **plate** (plates of ham = gam). **Brass** refers to an old term for a prostitute, 'flashtail', while *Billy Hunt*, shortened to **billy,** doesn't appear to have been a person, but probably recalls the obsolete slang term *billy-hunting*, which was used to describe the theft of both handkerchiefs and scrap metal.

Other terms are tantalizing. Is **Jimmy O'goblin** simply a made-up name designed to rhyme with *sovereign*, or is there an allusion to a character from nineteenth-century folklore or popular culture which is now lost? And is **barry,** for *Barry Nash*, a nod towards John Nash and Charles Barry, architects of London's Trafalgar Square?

Perhaps the best example an obscure point of reference preserved in rhyming slang is **chunder,** an Australian term popularized by Barry Humphries and the

Men at Work song *Down Under*. Chunder Foo of Akim Loo was a cartoon character used to sell Cobra Boot Polish in the early twentieth century. His full name provides a handy rhyme for *spew*, but as Chunder Foo himself is now little-known (and certainly less famous than his creator, the Australian artist Norman Lindsay), various false etymologies have sprung up for the *chunder*, including the theory that it was a contraction of 'Watch out under!', a cry supposedly made by those about to vomit from a higher deck onto a lower one on a ship.

jekyll and hydes *Australian* rhymes with *strides*, trousers: *let me get my jekyll and hydes on*

> The Strange Case of Dr Jekyll and Mr Hyde is a novella by Robert Louis Stevenson, published in 1886.

jersey flegg *Australian* keg, especially of beer: *they've got a few jersey fleggs in for tonight*

> Harry 'Jersey' Flegg was an Australian rugby league international and administrator.

jimmy (*Jimmy Grant*) *Australian* immigrant

> If this is a reference to a specific Jimmy Grant, he has long since been forgotten.

jimmy o'goblin *or* **jemmy o'goblin** sovereign (more recently, a pound)

jimmy riddle rhymes with *piddle* **1** urinate **2** act of urination

> Jimmy Riddle is unlikely to have been a real person.

joanna piano > *see* goanna

Joanna rhymes with the Cockney pronunciation *pianna*.

jodrell bank rhymes with [!] *wank*, act of masturbation: *'e's probably having a jodrell bank*

> The Jodrell Bank Observatory, in Cheshire, England, is an important centre of astronomical research.

joe baksi taxi: *we can jump in a joe baksi afterwards*

> Joe Baksi was a US heavyweight boxer who fought in London in 1946 and 1947.

joe blake *Australian* snake

joe blakes *Australian* rhymes with *shakes*, delirium tremens caused by an excess of alcohol: *I woke up with the joe blakes*

joe soap rhymes with *dope*, stupid or slow-witted person, often used ironically to refer to oneself: *so joe soap here ends up standing outside for half an hour, feeling a right charlie*

Mockneys

In recent years, rhyming slang has undergone a revival of sorts through the *mockney* phenomenon, which was first observed in the late 1980s. In the 1990s, films such as Guy Ritchie's *Lock, Stock, and Two Smoking Barrels* and Steven Soderbergh's *The Limey* popularized the trappings and traits of East End gangsters, who were themselves feted and celebrated in the 1960s. At the same time, various celebrities began to espouse working-class pursuits such as 'going down the dogs'. The result was a kind of 'geezer chic', in which a Cockney accent and liberal sprinkling of rhyming slang was at least as important as a natty **whistle.**

The mockneys – 'mock Cockneys'– have become a permanent fixture in British life, especially in the media. No upbringing is too privileged or geographically removed from London, it seems, to prevent certain individuals trying to pass themselves off as chirpy Cockney sparrows. And rhyming slang, especially if used with a straight face rather than the traditional wink, confers an extra degree of 'street' authenticity.

In fact, the speech patterns and posturing of the mockneys are highly artificial, recreating the East End fantasy of 70s gangster films and TV shows such as *The Sweeney* rather than any genuine

Cockney mode of speaking. It's an interesting kind of 'retro' fashion in language, but like other retro trends, it creates a heightened, exaggerated version of the original rather than anything close to it. But whatever else may be said for it, 'geezer chic' has undoubtedly given rhyming slang a new lease of life, and newly-coined rhymes such as **britneys, calvin,** and **brads** owe their existence to the mockneys.

john hop *Australian* rhymes with *cop*, police officer: *here come the john hops*

kate (*Kate Carney*) the British army: *'is manhole joined the kate*

> Kate Carney (1869–1950) was a music-hall entertainer known as the 'Cockney Queen'.

kate and sidney steak and kidney: *nothing beats a nice bit of kate and sidney* > see steak and kidney

kate mossed lost: *I'm kate mossed here*

> Kate Moss is a British model.

kembla (*Kembla Grange*) *Australian* small change: *Got any kembla for the meter?*

> Kembla Grange is a suburb of Wollongong, New South Wales, Australia.

ken dodd rhymes with *wad*, money: *you know the bloke – wears good whistles and always flashing his ken dodd around*

> Ken Dodd is a British comedian.

kermit (*Kermit the Frog*) rhymes with *bog*, lavatory: *'Scuse me – where's the kermit?*

> Kermit the Frog is the well-known amphibian host of *The Muppet Show*.

kerry packered *Australian* rhymes with *knackered*, tired; exhausted: *I'm still kerry packered from footie*

> Kerry Packer (1937–2005) was an Australian businessman who was the richest man in Australia at the time of his death.

khyber (*Khyber Pass*) rhymes with [!] *arse*, backside; anus

> The Khyber Pass is a historically and strategically important trade route between Afghanistan and Pakistan.

kingdom come rhymes with *bum*, backside: *give that lazy sherman a kick up the kingdom come*

kings (*kings and queens*) baked beans: *Fancy some kings on toast?*

kirribilli *Australian* silly: *that was a bit bloody kirribilli*

> Kirribilli is a suburb of Sydney, and contains the Australian prime minister's official Sydney residence.

lady godiva rhymes with *fiver*, five pounds: *I've only got a lady godiva to last me over the weekend*

> Lady Godiva is a semi-legendary medieval noblewoman who is said to have ridden naked through the streets of Coventry in protest at the taxes imposed by her husband.

lager lout rhymes with *kraut*, German person (both *kraut* and this sense of *lager lout* are highly offensive.)

lakes (*Lakes of Killarney*) rhymes with *barmy*, insane: *'e's bloody lakes, that bloke*

> The Lakes of Killarney, in County Kerry, Ireland, include Lough Leane.

lath (*lath and plaster*) master: *And what has the young lath to say for himself, then?*

lee marvin starving: *let's go for a basil – I'm lee marvin* > *see* hank marvin

> Lee Marvin (1924–1987) was a US film actor renowned for his tough-guy roles.

lemon (*lemon curd*) **1** rhymes with *bird*, woman **2** rhymes with [!] *turd*, piece of excrement

lemon and lime time: *I'd love to, darlin', if I 'ad the lemon and lime*

lemon squeezer rhymes with *geezer*, man: *ask the lemon squeezer at the bar*

leo (*Leo Sayer*) rhymes with *all-dayer*, all-day drinking session: *we was on another leo yesterday*

> Leo Sayer is an English pop singer.

lillian (*Lillian Gish*) **1** fish: *got some lillian for dinner tonight* **2** dish

> Lillian Gish (1893–1993) was a US cinema actress, a star of silent cinema known for her roles in *The Birth of a Nation, Duel in the Sun*, and *Night of the Hunter*.

linen (*linen draper*) newspaper: *Anything about it in the linen?*

loaf (*loaf of bread*) head: *Use your loaf!*

london taxi rhymes with [!] *jacksie* **1** backside: *'e wants a boot up the london taxi, that bloke* **2** anus: *she takes it up the london taxi*

lord mayor swear: *don't you lord mayor at me, you ship's anchor*

love and kisses rhymes with *missus,* wife or girlfriend: *regards to the love and kisses*

lucy locket pocket: *stick it in your lucy locket*

> *Lucy Locket* is an English nursery rhyme, the first line of which is 'Lucy Locket lost her pocket'.

lump of lead head

macaroni rhymes with *pony: short for pony and trap;* rhymes with [!] *crap,* act of defecation: *I'm bursting for a macaroni* > *see* pony

Named and shamed

Public figures always run the risk of having their names hijacked and given unwelcome rhyming associations. Thus Paul Weller and Uri Geller sometimes come in pints – as does Acker Bilk (though not in pubs!). Rhyming slang is no respecter of rank, as George Bush, Tony Blair, and Nelson Mandela have discovered. But at least they were spared the fate of Emma Freud and Belinda Carlisle, whose names are used to refer to a painful and embarrassing medical condition.

The fact is that a celebrity's character and deeds have no connection to the slang meanings that his or her name acquires. The silent-film actress ZaSu Pitts, for instance, did nothing in life to be permanently linked to diarrhoea. Of course, the whole point of rhyming slang is that the slang term should bear no obvious relation to its meaning. As a kind of *cant*, or secret language, rhyming slang depends on associations of sound rather than meaning. And anything – or anybody – is fair game.

The key to remaining anonymous (or at least relatively unscathed!) in slang terms is to ensure that your name affords no opportunities for rhymes that are scatological (Douglas Hurd), anatomical (Mal Meninga), or obscene

(Gary Glitter). So just what *was* James Blunt thinking when he changed his name from the relatively rhyme-safe Blount?

mad mick *Australian* rhymes with [!] *prick*, penis

mal meninga *Australian* finger; especially in the phrase 'give someone the finger', describing an obscene gesture or the sexual act that this gesture implies: *I just gave him the old mal meninga and walked off*

> 'Big' Mal Meninga was captain of the Australian Rugby League team from 1990 to 1994.

malcolm clift *Australian* lift: *Can you give us a malcolm clift?*

> Malcolm Clift was coach of the Canterbury Bulldogs rugby league team in the 1970s.

malky (*Malcolm Fraser*) *Scottish* razor: *a'm gonna gie that wee shite the malky*

> It has been suggested that Malcolm Fraser may have been a leader of one of Glasgow's 'razor gangs' in the 1930s.

mallee root *Australian* prostitute: *he was seeing a mallee root in town* See also **ron coote.**

> The mallee is a type of eucalyptus tree; its rootstock is used as fuel. *Root* is also Australian slang for a sexual partner.

manhole (*manhole cover*) brother: *saw your manhole down the battle*

> This rhyme only works with the Cockney pronunciation of 'brother' as *bruvva*.

mars and venus penis: *I 'eard 'e 'ad a problem with the old mars and venus*

mars bar *Scottish* scar: *I got that mars bar off a malkie*

> The Mars Bar™ is a popular chocolate and caramel confection. It looms large in the Scottish imagination, especially its deep-fried incarnation.

mary ellens rhymes with *melons*, breasts: *Seen the mary ellens on that?*

> Mary Ellen appears to be a name invented for the rhyme.

me and you menu: *What's on the me and you*

tonight, then?

> This rather weak rhyme is little more than a
> exaggerated pronunciation of 'menu', especially
> when ellided to 'me an' you'.

melvyn (*Melvyn Bragg*) rhymes with [!] *shag*, act
of sexual intercourse: *Fancy a melvyn?*

> Sir Melvyn Bragg is a British writer and
> broadcaster.

merry old soul rhymes with [!] *arsehole*,
despicable person: *'e's a merry old soul*

mickey (*Mickey Bliss*) rhymes with *piss*, urine,
especially in the phrase 'taking the piss': *'e's taking
the mickey*

> Mickey Bliss appears to be a name created for
> the rhyme.

mickey mouse rhymes with *Scouse*, Liverpudlian

> Mickey Mouse™ is an iconic cartoon character
> created by Walt Disney (1901–1966).

minces (*mince pies*) eyes: *wait till he gets his*

minces on this

miss or hit rhymes with [!] *shit,* act of defecation
> *see* hit or miss

monkey spanker rhymes with [!] *wanker,* foolish
person: *'e's a right monkey spanker, that one*

> *Monkey spanker* enjoys the happy position of
> being both rhyming slang and a direct reference
> to the act of masturbation ('spanking the
> monkey').

murray cod *Australian* rhymes with *nod,*
financial credit: *he's always buying things on the
murray cod*

> The Murray cod is a large Australian freshwater
> fish.

mystery bags *Australian* rhymes with *snags,*
slang for sausages: *sling a few mystery bags on the
barbie*

> This term is a nicely ironic comment on the
> dubious content of many sausages.

nanny goat 1 coat **2** boat **3** rhymes with *the Tote™*, the totalizator: a system of betting on horse races in which the aggregate stake, less an administration charge and tax, is paid out to winners in proportion to their stake

nav or **navvy** (*navigator*) rhymes with *tater*, potato: *Mum's roasting some navs for dinner*

> *Navvies*, or *navigators*, was a term originally for labourers who built canals or *navigations*.

ned kelly *Australian* **1** belly: *all I want is some tucker in me ned kelly and a good night's kip* **2** telly: *Anything on the ned kelly?*

> Ned Kelly (1855–1880) was a famous bushranger, best known for his armour-clad last stand against the police before his capture and execution.

needle (*needle and pin*) gin: *pint of apple and a needle and tonic, please*

needle and thread bread

Ned Kelly = telly

nellie *or* **nelly** **1** (*Nellie Deane*) rhymes with [!] *queen*, gay man: *the place was full of nellies* **2** (*Nellie Duff*) rhymes with [!] *puff*, gay man: *Your mate – is he a nelly?* **3** (*Nellie Duff*) rhymes with *puff*, breath, life: *not on your nellie*

> Nellie Deane is a character in a music-hall song; Nellie Duff is probably a name invented for the rhyme.

nelson (*Nelson Mandela*) rhymes with *Stella*, Stella Artois™, a popular brand of Belgian lager: *let's get down the rubbity and neck a few nelsons* > *see* paul weller, uri

> The name of the South African statesman handily rhymes with Stella.

noah (*Noah's Ark*) *Australian* shark: *there's noahs out by the reef*

nobbies (*Nobby Stiles*) piles (haemorrhoids): *me bleedin' nobbies is causing me no end of discomfort*

> Norbert Stiles MBE is a footballer who played for England in the 1966 World Cup final.

Noah (Noah's ark) = shark

north and south mouth: *Shut yer north and south!*

nose and chin win: *I 'ad a good nose and chin on the airs and graces*

ocean wave shave: *I'd no time to even have an ocean wave this morning*

oliver (*Oliver Twist*) rhymes with [!] *pissed*, drunk: *I was well oliver by the time I left the rubbity*

> *Oliver Twist* (1838) is one of Charles Dickens' best-known novels.

ones and twos shoes: *I got a brilliant bargain on a pair of ones and twos this morning*

orchestra stalls rhymes with [!] *balls*, testicles

Oscar (*Oscar Asche*) *Australian* cash

> Oscar Asche (1871–1936) was an Australian actor.

oxo (*OXO™ cube*) rhymes with *Tube™*, the

London Underground: *take the oxo to Bethnal Green*

pat (*Pat Malone*) *Australian* alone, own: *I'm on me pat tonight* > *see* tod

> Pat Malone is the subject of an Australian folk song.

paul weller rhymes with *Stella*, Stella Artois™, a popular brand of Belgian lager > *see* nelson, uri

> Paul Weller is a British rock musician.

pearly (*pearly king*) rhymes with [!] *ring*, anus: *my pearly was on fire after that ruby*

> A pearly king is a London costermonger who wears a traditional costume covered with pearl buttons.

peckham (*Peckham Rye*) tie: *I'm wearing a whistle and a red peckham*

> Peckham Rye is a South London railway station.

pen and ink rhymes with *stink*, fuss: *there was a*

bit of a pen and ink about the office move

pete tong wrong: *it's all gone pete tong*

> Pete Tong is a British dance-music DJ.

pipe (*pipe and drum*) rhymes with *bum,* backside:
I've been sitting on me pipe all day

pitch (*pitch-and-toss*) boss: *there's no way the
pitch'll give me the time off*

> Pitch-and-toss is a game of skill and chance
> played with coins.

plate fellate: *'e got 'imself plated by a brass*

> While *plate* rhymes with *fellate,* it's actually short
> for *plates of ham.* This rhymes with *gam,* an
> obsolete slang word for the action that derives
> from the French *gamahucher.*

plates of meat feet

polish (*polish and gloss*) rhymes with [!] *toss,*
masturbate; act of masturbation: *when 'e finally
went to the brass, all 'e could afford was a polish*

> This term neatly combines a rhyme with a fairly
> obvious sexual metaphor.

pony (*pony and trap*) rhymes with [!] *crap,* act of defecation

porky (*pork pie*) lie: *porkies, mate, you're telling porkies*

posh'n'becks sex: *'e 'asn't 'ad any posh'n'becks for six month*

> David Beckham was England football captain
> from 2000 to 2006. His wife Victoria was known
> as Posh Spice when a member of the pop group
> The Spice Girls.

potato (*potato peeler*) *Australian* rhymes with *sheila,* woman: *that's a potato's drink, mate – you'll be wanting a shandy next*

> Germaine Greer famously objected to this term
> in *The Female Eunuch.*

rabbit (*rabbit and pork*) talk: *just listen to me rabbiting on*

This rhyme depends on the Cockney pronunciation of 'talk' as *tork*.

racquel welch belch: *the nelsons always make me racquel welch*

> Racquel Welch is an American actress, best known for wearing a fur bikini in the film *One Million Years BC*.

rag and bone rhymes with *throne*, toilet: *I was sitting on the rag and bone*

raleigh bike™ rhymes with [!] *dyke*, lesbian: *I don't believe she's a raleigh bike*

raspberry (*raspberry ripple*) rhymes with *cripple*, disabled person: *'elp 'im with the door – poor geezer's a raspberry*

raspberry (*raspberry tart*) rhymes with [!] *fart*, emission of intestinal gas from the anus, esp an audible one: *and then she let out a massive raspberry*

raspberry (tart) = fart

ravi shankar rhymes with [!] *wanker*, foolish or contemptible person: *what a complete ravi shankar*

> Ravi Shankar is a world-famous sitar player.

reggie (*reggie and ronnie*) rhymes with *johnny*, condom: *that's fine, as long as you use a reggie*

> Reginald (1933–2000) and Ronald Kray (1933–1995) were identical twin gangsters who terrorized the East End of London in the 1960s.

reginalds (*Reg Grundies*) *Australian* rhymes with *undies*, underwear: *she answered the door in her reginalds*

> Reg Grundy is an Australian media mogul.

richard (*Richard III*) rhymes with *bird*, woman: *Who's the richard?*

> Richard III (1452–1485), king of England (1483–1485), is notorious as the suspected murderer of his two young nephews in the Tower of London.

rinky-dink rhymes with *Chink*, Chinese person:

she married a rinky-dink (Both *rinky-dink* and *Chink* are highly offensive terms.)

river ouse rhymes with *booze,* alcoholic drinks: *we're gonna hit the old river ouse tonight, my son*

> The Ouse is a river in North Yorkshire.

rock (*rock of ages*) **wages:** *got me rock in me back pocket – going down the battle*

rock and roll rhymes with *dole,* unemployment benefit: *I've been back on the old rock and roll for the last six months*

rogan (*rogan josh*) rhymes with *dosh,* money: *that'll set you back a fair bit of rogan*

> Rogan josh is an Indian dish made with tomatoes, meat, and red peppers.

rogue (*rogue and villain*) shilling: *that'll cost you a rogue*

> A shilling was a coin worth one twentieth of a pound in predecimal British currency.

ron coote *Australian* rhymes with *root,* sexual partner or sexual intercourse: *I'm after a ron coote tonight*

> Ron Coote is a former Australian rugby league international.

rosie (*Rosie Lee*) tea: *sit yourself down and we'll have a cup of rosie*

> Although the rhyme is often thought to come from Gypsy Rose Lee (1911-1970), the famous burlesque artiste and actress, the expression, also found as Rosie Lea, was current in the late 19th century. Its real origin is unknown.

rubbity or **rubbidy** (*rubbity dub*) pub: *see you down the rubbity tonight*

> *Rubbity* is a corruption of *rub-a-dub-dub,* from the opening line of the nursery rhyme: *Rub-a-dub-dub, three men in a tub.*

ruby (*Ruby Murray*) curry: *Fancy going up Brick Lane for a ruby?*

> Ruby Murray (1935–1996) was a Belfast-born singer noted for her hoarse voice.

salmon (*salmon and trout*) rhymes with *snout*, tobacco: *Got any snout on ya?*

> 'Snout' has been established as a slang term for tobacco or cigarettes since the nineteenth century.

salvador dali *Scottish* rhymes with *swalley, a Scottish form of swallow,* drink: *let's have a wee salvador dali*

> The Spanish artist Salvador Dali (1904–1989) was a leading figure in the surrealist movement.

sausage (*sausage and mash*) cash: *I ain't got a sausage on me* > *see* bangers

saveloy boy: *'e's a nice saveloy, but a bit thick*

scarper leave, escape

> *Scarper* may be derived from Italian *scappare*, but may also hail from rhyming slang *Scapa Flow*, 'go'. The rhyme only works with the Cockney pronunciation of *Scapa*, with a long *a* and an *r* sound at the end.

scoob (*Scooby-Doo*) clue: *sorry, don't have a scoob*

Scooby-Doo™ is the eponymous canine star of a popular cartoon series that was produced by Hanna-Barbera studios.

scotch (*Scotch egg*) leg: *look at the scotches on that geezer*

A Scotch egg is a hard-boiled egg enclosed in a layer of sausage meat, covered in egg and breadcrumbs, and fried.

scotch mist rhymes with [!] *pissed*, drunk: *feeling slightly scotch mist*

selina (*Selina Scott*) spot, blemish, or pimple: *you should do something about your selinas*

Selina Scott is a British TV presenter.

septic (*septic tank*) rhymes with *Yank*, American person: *this septic come into the rubbity last night*

sexton (*Sexton Blake*) fake: *don't believe a word that sexton says*

Sexton Blake is a fictional detective created by Harry Blyth ('Hal Meredith') in 1893.

Polari

One of the ways in which rhyming slang functions is as a kind of secret language or *cant*. It's unsurprising, therefore, that elements of rhyming slang were incorporated into one of the more enduring English cants, Polari, or Parlyarlee.

Polari is an intriguing mixture of Italian, Romany, backslang, rhyming slang, and other languages. It may have its origins in the Lingua Franca of the Mediterranean ports, a hybrid language that combined elements of Italian, Occitan, Arabic, Greek, and Turkish. English sailors appear to have learned this and brought it back to the British Isles, where it was used by travelling folk and showmen. The Italian elements, including the name of the cant (from *parlare* 'to talk'), were probably strengthened in the nineteenth century by an influx of entertainers from Italy. The cant then became associated with the theatre and its patrons and players.

In the twentieth century, Polari was mainly used by gay men, and served as a surreptitious means of identifying potential sexual partners – at a time when homosexual acts were illegal. It's unsurprising, therefore, that Polari has a particular, and indeed mechanical, emphasis on sexual acts and the pertinent body parts, and so includes many of the saucier terms from the rhyming lexicon, such as **plate, arthur, barclays,** and **steamer.**

In its gay incarnation, Polari was the language of furtive encounters in parks and public toilets – a world in which any potential *trade* could be a front for the *sharpies*, or police, and in which discretion was essential. But with the decriminalization of homosexual acts in 1967, the need for the cant began to vanish. The popularity of the BBC radio comedy show *Round the Horne*, in which Hugh Paddick and Kenneth Williams played the extremely camp, Polari-speaking couple Julian and Sandy, also helped to demystify it. Thus, despite attempts to revive it in recent years, Polari has all but vanished apart from a few words such as *naff*, *drag*, and *ponce*, and the rhyming slang that it helped to perpetuate in the twentieth century.

sharp (*sharp and blunt*) rhymes with [!] *cunt*
1 female genitals 2 women considered sexually:
I'm after a bit of sharp tonight

sherman (*sherman tank*) rhymes with [!] *wank*
1 act of masturbation 2 foolish or contemptible
person: *you're such a sherman*

> A Sherman tank was a US-produced armoured
> vehicle in World War II.

ship's anchor rhymes with [!] *wanker,* foolish or
contemptible person

shovel (*shovel and pick*) rhymes with *mick,*
Irishman (*Shovel, shovel and pick,* and *mick* are
highly offensive terms.)

> Shovel plays on the perception of Irish
> immigrants as manual labourers.

shovel (*shovel and broom*) room: *you can rent the*
shovel at the back

side of beef *Scottish* rhymes with *deif,* deaf: *Are*

ye side of beef, ye wee bastard? > *see* corned beef

> This rhyme depends on the pronunciation of
> 'deaf' as *deef* in some Scottish dialects.

sigourney (*Sigourney Weaver*) rhymes with [!]
beaver, the female genitals; female pubic hair: *I
just had my sigourney waxed. God, it hurt.*

> Sigourney Weaver is a US actress renowned for
> her portrayal of Ripley in the *Alien* series of
> films.

silver spoon 1 moon: *we danced all bleedin' night
by the light of the silver spoon* **2** *Australian* rhymes
with *hoon,* hooligan: *it's full of silver spoons down
there*

> *Hoon* is an Australian slang term of unknown
> origin.

silvery moon rhymes with *coon,* Black person
(Both *silvery moon* and *coon* are highly offensive
terms.)

sir anthony (*Sir Anthony Blunt*) rhymes with [!]

cunt, mean or obnoxious person: *you won't get any help from that sir anthony over there*

> Anthony Blunt (1907–1983) was a British art historian and traitor who spied for the Soviet Union.

skin and blister sister: *the lemon's 'is skin and blister*

sky rocket pocket: *time to stick yer 'and in the old sky rocket, my son*

squid quid (£1): *lend us a squid*

steak and kidney *Australian* Sydney: *my sister lives in steak and kidney* > see kate and sidney

steamer (*steam tug*) rhymes with *mug,* client of a male prostitute: *don't mind 'im, dear – just one of me steamers*

> This term was frequently used in Polari.

steffi (*Steffi Graf*) laugh: *'e's 'aving a steffi, mate*

> Steffi Graf is a German tennis player.

stick of rock rhymes with [!] *cock*, penis: *Like sweets, darling? I've got a stick of rock ...*

> Like many examples of sexual rhyming slang, this functions as a none-too-subtle metaphor as well.

stoke (*Stoke-on-Trent*) rhymes with [!] *bent*, gay: *'e's stoke, innit*

> Stoke-on-Trent is a city in the Midlands, England.

sweaty (*sweaty sock*) rhymes with *jock*, Scotsman: *can't believe the sweaties turned us over*

sweeney (*Sweeney Todd*) flying squad: a former name for the Metropolitan Police Force's Serious Robbery Squad

> Sweeney Todd is the fictional 'demon barber of Fleet Street', a murderer who turns his victims into meat pies. The rhyming term was popularized by the 1970s TV series *The Sweeney*.

syrup (*syrup of fig*) wig: *that geezer's wearing a syrup*

Syrup of fig is used as a sweetener, cocktail mixer, and laxative.

tart (*tom tart*) rhymes with *sweetheart,* prostitute > *see* tom

The origins of the term *tart* are somewhat obscure; at some point it seems simply to have been short for *sweetheart* (meaning simply 'girlfriend'), while at other times *tom tart* has been used as a rhyming – and euphemistic – phrase for *sweetheart,* meaning 'prostitute'.

taters (*taters in the mould*) cold: *It's bloody taters out there!*

tea leaf thief: *watch your wallet – there's a tea leaf about*

teddy bear *Australian* rhymes with *lair,* flashy man who shows off: *he's a bit of a teddy bear, that one*

Lair is a common Australian slang term.

thrups (*thrupenny bits*) rhymes with [!] tits,

breasts: *plenty of thrups on show*

tiddler (*tiddlywink*) drink: *You up for a tiddler or two tonight?*

tin lid Australian kid: *I'll drop the tin lids off*

tin tack sack: *she got the tin tack last week*

titfer (*tit for tat*) hat: *Where's me titfer?*

to and from Australian rhymes with *pom*, British person: *she's going out with this to and from*

tod (*Tod Sloan*) own, alone: *she's on her tod today* > *see* pat

> Tod Sloan (1874–1933) was a famous US jockey.

tom (*tom tart*) rhymes with *sweetheart*, prostitute: *they're all toms* > *see* tart

> *Sweetheart* is here a euphemism for a prostitute.

tom and dick sick: *she's been tom and dick all week*

tom and jerry rhymes with *merry*, drunk: *'e's a bit*

tom and jerry

Tom and Jerry™ are, respectively, a cat and mouse locked in an eternal struggle in the cartoon series produced by Metro-Goldwyn-Mayer.

tomfoolery jewellery: *she's all done up with tomfoolery*

tommy rollocks rhymes with [!] *bollocks,* testicles: *she's got him by the tommy rollocks*

toms (*tomtits*) *Australian* rhymes with [!] *shits,* diarrhoea: *I got the toms from those shrimps*

Tom tit is another name for the bluetit.

tom sawyer lawyer

The Adventures of Tom Sawyer is an 1876 novel by Mark Twain.

tom tank rhymes with [!] *wank,* act of masturbation: *off to uncle ted for a tom tank*

Tom Tank is unlikely to have been a real person.

tonies (*Tony Blairs*) flares: *'e looks ridiculous in them tonies*

tony blair hair: *don't like 'is tony blair much*

trevor (*Trevor Nunn*) rhymes with 2:1, upper-second honours degree > *see* attila, desmond, douglas, geoff

> Trevor Nunn is a British theatre director.

trolley (*trolley and truck*) rhymes with [!] *fuck*, act of sexual intercourse: *What's a gel gotta do to get a trolley round 'ere?*

> This rhyme gave rise to the picturesque term 'trolley-oggling', for voyeurism.

trouble and strife wife: *better see what the trouble and strife has to say about it*

tumbledown (*tumble down the sink*) drink: *Fancy a tumbledown after work?*

tuppenny (*tuppenny loaf*) rhymes with *loaf of*

bread, head: *I can't get me tuppenny around this*
> see loaf

> 'Tuppenny', or 'two-penny', has long been used
> to mean 'cheap or tawdry'.

turkish (*Turkish bath*) laugh: *you're having a turkish*

turtle (*turtle dove*) glove: *don't forget your weasel and turtles*

twist (*twist and twirl*) girl: *she's a nice-looking twist*

two and eight state: *'E gets himself into a right two and eight*

> 'Two and eight' would be two shillings, eight
> pence in predecimal British currency.

two by four rhymes with *whore*, prostitute: *'is missus found the number of a two by four on 'is mobile*

two-wheeler *Australian* rhymes with *sheila*, woman: *Who's the two-wheeler with Dave?*

103

two - wheeler = sheila

uncle and aunt plant (of the garden or house variety): *'e spends all 'is time in the garden with his uncles and aunts*

uncle bob rhymes with [!] *knob*, penis: *'e can't keep 'is uncle bob in 'is trousers*

uncle fester child molester: *you want to keep the god forbids away from 'im – 'e looks a right uncle fester* > *see* uncle lester

> Uncle Fester is a member of the ghoulish Addams Family created by US cartoonist Charles Addams.

uncle lester child molester: *watch out – uncle lester's about* > *see* uncle fester

> This rhyme perhaps draws on the 'creepy uncle' figure of popular folklore.

uncle mac rhymes with *smack*, heroin: *she's been on the uncle mac for years*

uncle ted bed: *I'm going to uncle ted*

uncle wilf rhymes with *filth*, police: *let's scarper before uncle wilf gets here*

up and under *Australian* rhymes with *chunder*, vomit: *Mick's in the bog having an up and under* > *see* chunder

uri (*Uri Geller*) rhymes with *Stella*, Stella Artois™, a popular brand of Belgian lager: *we 'ad a few pints of uri last night* > *see* nelson, paul weller

> Uri Geller is an Israeli broadcaster and author with an interest in the paranormal.

vera lynn 1 gin: *a vera lynn for me please, love* **2** chin: *'e caught it right on 'is vera lynn* **3** rhymes with *skin*, cigarette paper: *Got any vera lynns on you?*

> The popular singer Dame Vera Lynn was known as 'The Forces' Sweetheart' during the Second World War.

von trapp rhymes with [!] *crap*, act of defecation:

off for a von trapp

> The Von Trapps were a famous Austrian singing family who inspired the hit Broadway musical and 1965 film *The Sound of Music*.

wallace and gromit vomit: *I saw him in the bog having a right old wallace and gromit*

> Wallace and Gromit are the popular creations of Oscar-winning British animator Nick Park.

wally (*Wally Grout*) *Australian* rhymes with *shout*, round (of drinks): *What are you and the sheilas having? It's my wally.*

> Arthur Theodore Wallace 'Wally' Grout (1927–1968) played cricket for Queensland and Australia.

weasel (*weasel and stoat*) coat: *get yer weasel – you've pulled*

weaver's (*weaver's chair*) prayer, especially in the sense of a chance or hope: *you ain't got a weaver's, mate*

weasel (& stoat) = coat

wee georgie (*Wee Georgie Wood*) good: *that was wee georgie, I thought*

> Wee Georgie Wood (1894–1979) was a diminutive star of the music hall.

wentworth falls *Australian* rhymes with [!] *balls*, testicles: *we've got him by the wentworth falls*

> Wentworth Falls is a village in the Blue Mountains, New South Wales, Australia, named after nearby waterfalls.

werris (*Werris Creek*) rhymes with *leak*, act of urination: *Excuse me – gotta take a werris*

> Werris Creek is a small town in New South Wales, Australia.

west hams (*West Ham reserves*) nerves: *'e gets on my west hams, that bloke*

> West Ham United is an East London football club.

whistle (*whistle and flute*) suit: *check out the whistle on that geezer*

widow twankey 1 hanky: *Can I borrow your widow twankey?* **2** rhymes with *Yankee*, American person

> In the pantomime *Aladdin*, 'Widow Twankey' is the hero's mother.

wilkie (*Wilkie Bard*) card: *I'm brassic after that night on the wilkies*

> Wilkie Bard (1874–1944) was a music-hall singer and pantomime star known for his hit song *She Sells Sea Shells*.

winona (*Winona Ryder*) cider: *pint of winona, please*

> Winona Ryder is an American actress who starred in films such as *Heathers* and *Beetlejuice*.

woolly woofter *Australian* rhymes with [!] *poofter*, homosexual man: *Soccer's a game for poms and woolly woofters, mate!*

wyatt earp burp: *this stuff makes you wyatt earp*

> Wyatt Earp (1848–1929) was a US lawman, famed for his participation in the gunfight at the OK Corral in 1881.

The Music Hall

The music-hall tradition of the late nineteenth and early twentieth centuries plays a major part in the history of British popular culture – and in the development of rhyming slang. The first 'music halls' in the mid-nineteenth century were pub rooms in which a variety of musical and comic entertainments were provided.

Later in the Victorian period, purpose-built music halls sprang up, and became a central aspect of working-class culture in British cities, especially London. The entertainment on offer was always lively, often risqué, and rooted in the experiences of ordinary people.

Unsurprisingly, many of the stars of music hall have been immortalized in rhyme. Examples include Kate Carney (**kate**), Wilkie Bard (**wilkies**), Harry Randall (**harry**), and **Wee Georgie Wood.** But the influence of the music hall on rhyming slang goes beyond the provision of celebrity ammunition for rhymers.

Singers such as Albert Chevalier and Marie Lloyd used rhyming slang in their stage favourites, popularizing – and in some cases inventing – rhymes in their lyrics. Many rhyming slang terms are as much a product of the music-hall stage as the streets of London's East End, and the emphasis on innuendo and sauciness in much of the material created a fertile atmosphere for the nod-and-wink of rhyming slang. As music-hall songs formed the basis for the 'knees-up', that staple of Cockney home entertainment, the patter and humour of the stars melded seamlessly with the speech of the streets.

ying yang rhymes with [!] *wang,* penis

you and me tea: *let's have a cup of you and me*

zane grey *Australian* pay: *I can't go out until Wednesday, when I get my zane grey*

> Zane Grey (1872–1939) was a US pulp-fiction writer known for his westerns such as *Riders of the Purple Sage.*

zasu pitts rhymes with [!] *shits,* diarrhoea: *Jesus! Think I've got the zasu pitts!*

> ZaSu Pitts (1894–1963) was a US film actress.

zorba (*Zorba the Greek*) rhymes with *take a leak,* urinate: *I'll zorba before we go in*

> *Zorba the Greek* is a 1952 novel by Nikos Kazantzakis, which was filmed in 1964.